The salty sea air,
the wind blowing in your face.

PRINCE ERIC: *King Triton?*

SAILOR: *Ruler of the merpeople.*

GRIMSBY:

Merpeople!

Eric, pay no attention to this nautical nonsense.

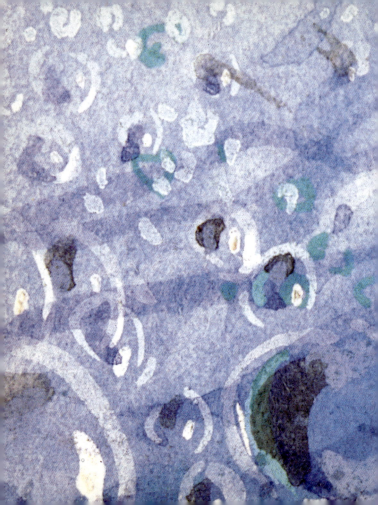

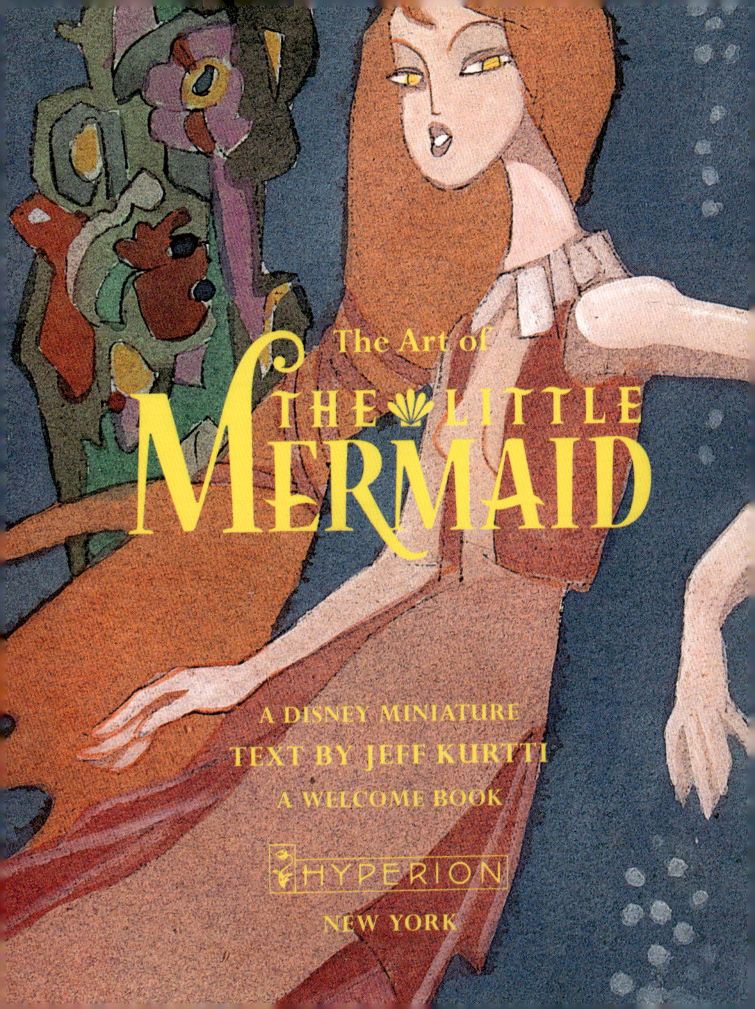

The Art of

THE LITTLE MERMAID

A DISNEY MINIATURE

TEXT BY JEFF KURTTI

A WELCOME BOOK

HYPERION

NEW YORK

Adapted from Walt Disney Pictures'
The Little Mermaid
Written and Directed by John Musker and Ron Clements
Produced by Howard Ashman and John Musker
Lyrics by Howard Ashman
Music by Alan Menken
© 1988 Walt Disney Music Company and Wonderland Music Company, Inc.
International Copyright Secured. All Rights Reserved. Used by Permission.

For information, address Hyperion
114 Fifth Avenue, New York, NY 10011

ISBN 0-7868-6335-8
"A Disney Miniature" Edition

Produced by Welcome Enterprises, Inc.
588 Broadway, New York, NY 10012

Designed by Davidson Design, New York
Photography by Michael Stern
Printed and bound in Singapore by Toppan Printing Co., Inc.

10 9 8 7 6 5 4 3 2 1

Contents

Once upon a time in a kingdom beneath the sea, there lived a beautiful mermaid princess named Ariel, who dreamed of being a part of the human world. One day, her father, King Triton, held a gala concert. The symphony, written by his majesty's court composer, Sebastian, would feature Triton's daughters Aquata, Andrina, Arista, Attina, Adella, and Alana as well as the musical debut of Ariel. But when the time came for her entrance, Ariel was nowhere to be found. Her daydreams of the world above the waves had distracted the little mermaid again.

SEBASTIAN:

*Your Majesty, this will be the finest
concert I ever conducted.*

$\mathcal{F}$ar away from the musical celebration, Ariel and her best friend, Flounder, explored the rotting hulk of a human shipwreck, in search of unusual treasures of the human world to add to Ariel's secret collection. Even the menacing sharks that haunted such forgotten places couldn't keep Ariel from her quest. Some of the objects she found puzzled the little mermaid. What could these peculiar things be used for? Ariel swam to the surface to ask the seagull Scuttle to identify her new-found treasures.

FLOUNDER:

Ariel, wait for me!

ARIEL:

Flounder! Hurry up!...Isn't it fantastic!

Oh, my gosh! Have you ever seen anything
so wonderful in your life?

FLOUNDER.

Cool! But what is it?

FLOUNDER:

Did you hear something?

ARIEL:

Flounder, relax. Nothing is going to happen.

FLOUNDER:

Sharks! Swim! A shark!

ARIEL:

Scuttle! Look what we found.

FLOUNDER:

Human stuff.

SCUTTLE:

It's a dingelhopper.
Humans use these little babies to straighten their hair.

SCUTTLE:

This I haven't seen in years.
The snarfblatt dates back to prehysterical times...

...they invented the snarfblatt to make music...

*Music! The concert!
My gosh!*

My father's gonna kill me!

When Ariel returned to Triton's undersea palace, her father was furious at her absence. And when Flounder accidentally revealed that he and Ariel had been to the surface again, his royal temper boiled over. Triton tried to make his daughter understand that the human world and the mer-world could never meet, and that her dreams of life above the sea were dangerous. Frustrated by her father's lack of understanding, Ariel left Triton and swam to her secret grotto of human treasures. Poor Triton, worried for his daughter's safety, appointed Sebastian to keep an eye on her.

TRITON:

As long as you live under my ocean, obey my rules!
I am never to hear of you going to the surface again. Clear?

*Teenagers!…Give them an inch,
they swim all over you.*

TRITON:

She needs constant supervision....
And you are just the crab to do it.

Look at
this trove,
treasures untold...

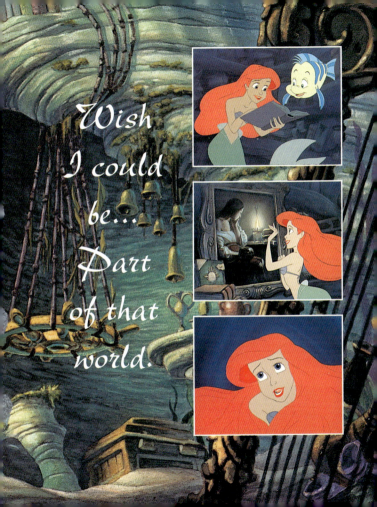

Wish I could be... Part of that world.

While the little mermaid sadly considered her gloomy predicament, the bright flash of fireworks far above the waves caught her attention. Ariel rose to the surface to see what was happening. She saw a handsome prince on board a passing ship, and fell in love at first sight. As Ariel gazed longingly at the handsome Prince Eric, a sudden and furious storm arose, sweeping him overboard. Rescuing Eric, Ariel carried him safely to shore, singing to him as he came back to consciousness. When the prince awakened, Ariel dove out of sight, leaving him only the haunting memory of her lovely voice.

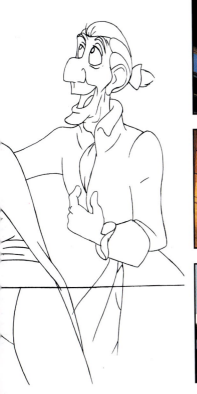

PRINCE ERIC:

She's out there somewhere...When I find her, I'll know. It'll just hit me like lightning.

SAILOR:

Hurricane a-coming!

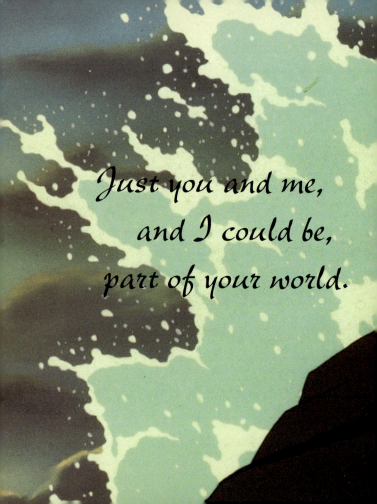

Just you and me,
and I could be,
part of your world.

*A*riel was in love. The sea king was overjoyed! Maybe Ariel's affection for this unknown mer-man would stop her vexing fascination with human non-sense. Sebastian tried unsuccessfully to convince Ariel to forget Prince Eric. When Triton discovered Ariel's secret grotto, and that the object of her affections was a human, the sea king was furious. He destroyed Ariel's treasures and commanded his daughter to forget the human at once! Slithering in the shadows, two menacing eels calmly observed the clash. The eels, Flotsam and Jetsam, were the companions of the evil sea witch Ursula.

ATTINA: *She's got it bad.*

TRITON: *What has she got?*

ANDRINA:

Isn't it obvious, Daddy? Ariel's in love.

ARIEL:

I've got to see him again.

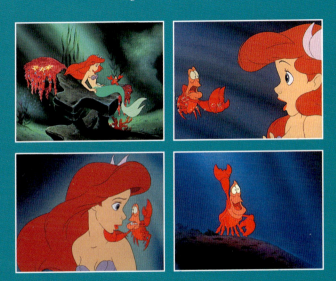

SEBASTIAN: *Get your head out of the clouds and back in the water. Down here is your home!*

Under the Sea. Darlin' it's better down where it's wetter. Take it from me.

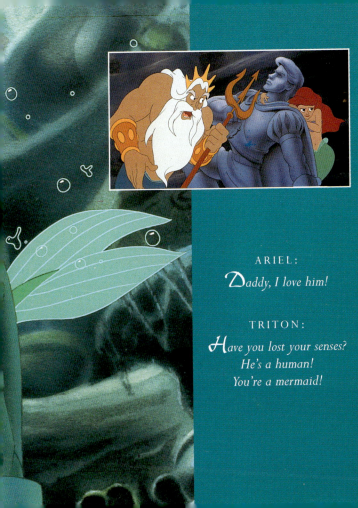

ARIEL:

Daddy, I love him!

TRITON:

Have you lost your senses?
He's a human!
You're a mermaid!

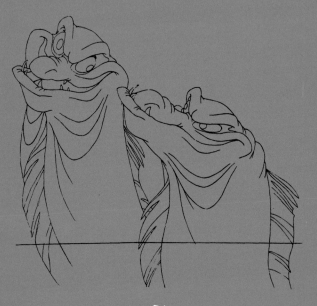

FLOTSAM: *Poor child.*

JETSAM: *We represent someone who...*

FLOTSAM: *...Can make all your dreams come true.*

Determined to be with her prince, Ariel went to call upon the sea witch for help. The scheming outcast Ursula saw her chance to exact revenge on King Triton and was more than willing to cooperate. Now, if the little mermaid would simply sacrifice her voice to the sea witch, she would gladly cast a magic spell to give Ariel human form. But, if Prince Eric did not kiss her by the end of three days' time, Ariel would return to her original form, and become Ursula's slave forever! Despite the protests of her companions, the smitten mermaid agreed to Ursula's terrible bargain, and the spell was cast.

URSULA: *It's what I live for....*
To help unfortunate merfolk, like yourself.
Poor souls with no one else to turn to.

*I'll make a potion that will turn you into
a human for three days. Before the sun sets
on the third day... he's got to kiss you.*

Go ahead, make your choice. It won't cost much. Just your voice.

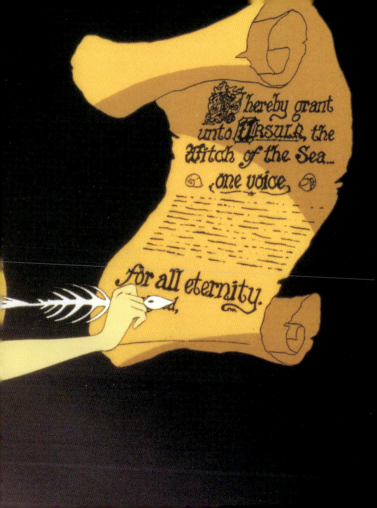

*I*n human form,

Ariel could not swim, so her friends carried her to shore. There, ragged and mute, she was found by Eric, who took her to his palace. Despite his misgivings, Sebastian followed her and narrowly escaped becoming crab *cordon bleu* in the palace kitchen.

As Eric proudly escorted Ariel through his kingdom, he found her strangely familiar and thoroughly enchanting. But he could not give up his dream of finding the mysterious young woman whose haunting voice had awakened him on shore. Unable to speak, Ariel waited and hoped that Eric would realize that she was the selfsame young woman.

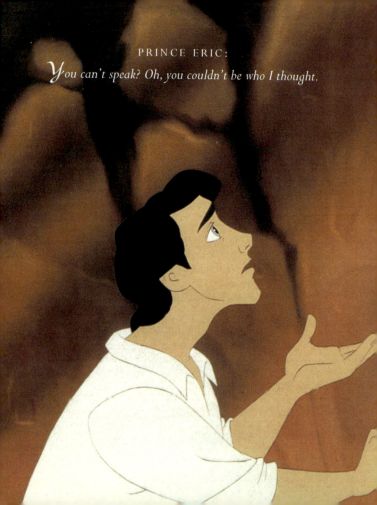

PRINCE ERIC:

You can't speak? Oh, you couldn't be who I thought.

Les poissons, les poissons,

How I love les poissons.

As the second day ended, Sebastian finally took matters into his own claws, and conducted an encouragaing serenade as Ariel and Eric drifted in a rowboat over a romantic moonlit lagoon. Success seemed just a kiss away, but Ursula had no intention of letting Ariel slip through her tentacles. Just as the spell-breaking kiss seemed near at hand, Flotsam and Jetsam rose from the depths, overturning the little boat and drenching the romantic mood.

FLOUNDER:

Has he kissed her?

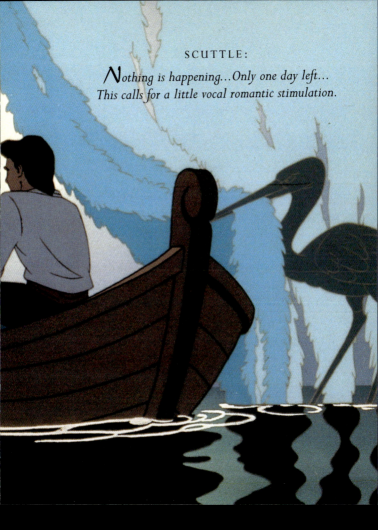

SCUTTLE:

Nothing is happening…Only one day left…
This calls for a little vocal romantic stimulation.

You've gotta kiss the girl.

Go on and kiss the girl.

URSULA:

That was a close one. Too close. It's time I took matters into my own tentacles.

Ursula realized that Ariel might succeed in fulfilling her end of the bargain, so the sea witch disguised herself as a beautiful maiden named Vanessa, and lured Eric to her side, spellbinding the young prince with Ariel's stolen voice. All seemed lost for Ariel as Eric and Vanessa prepared to wed on board a cheerful wedding ship. Then Scuttle brought the dejected Ariel big news! He had discovered Vanessa's true identity.

The bride-to-be was actually the sea witch in disguise!

GRIMSBY:
...*It appears
I was mistaken.
This mystery maiden of
yours...does in fact exist.*

PRINCE ERIC:
*We wish to be married
right away.
The wedding ship
departs at sunset.*

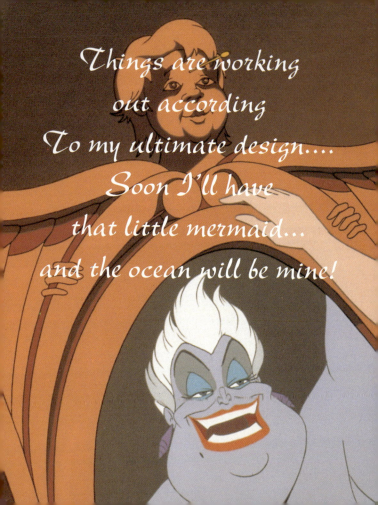

Things are working
out according
To my ultimate design....
Soon I'll have
that little mermaid...
and the ocean will be mine!

SCUTTLE:

The prince is marrying the sea witch in disgiuse!

*A*lerted, Ariel's friends stopped the wedding and tricked Ursula into revealing herself. But Ursula could not be conquered so easily. Without Eric's kiss as the sun set, Ariel fell into the clutches of the sea witch. It seemed the hapless merprincess would be lost forever.

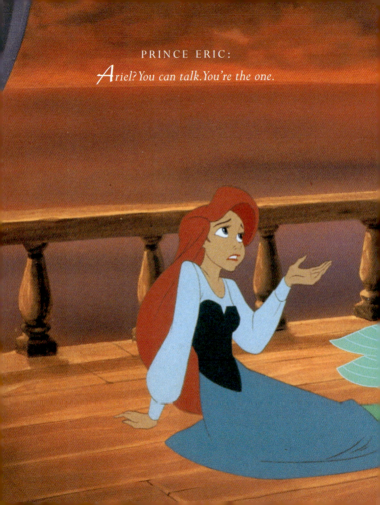

PRINCE ERIC:

Ariel? You can talk. You're the one.

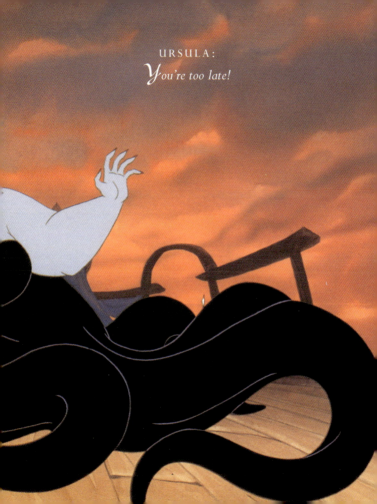

URSULA:

You're too late!

Then, in a selfless act of love for his daughter, Triton offered to take his daughter's place in Ursula's wicked bargain. Ursula gleefully agreed, gloatingly turned Triton into a wretched, powerless soul, and pilfered his crown, trident, and magic powers.

The sea witch wrenched the terrified Ariel away from Eric, vanishing with the little mermaid into the depths of the ocean.

URSULA:

*Poor Princess.
I'm not after you.
I've much bigger
fish to fry.*

ARIEL:

Daddy, I'm sorry!

URSULA:

The contract's legal, binding and completely unbreakable. But...I might be willing to make an exchange. For someone even better.

Determined to save
Ariel, Eric battled the
powers of Ursula's evil
magic in a thunderous clash
on a storm-tossed sea. The
courageous prince vanquished
the crowing sea witch, and saved Triton and
Ariel from their doom.

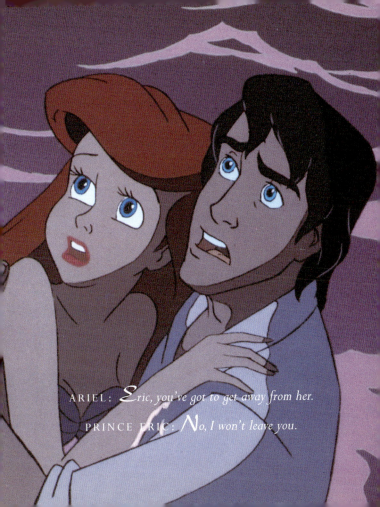

ARIEL: *Eric, you've got to get away from her.*

PRINCE ERIC: *No, I won't leave you.*

$\mathcal{W}$ith everyone safe at last, King Triton soberly restored Ariel's human form, allowing her marriage to Eric. With the sea king's poignant blessing, Ariel bid good-bye to her home under the sea, and sailed with her new love into the adventure of a new life.

KING TRITON:

She really does love him, doesn't she, Sebastian?
Then I guess there's just one problem left.
How much I'm going to miss her.

History

"I think our films have brought new adult respect for the fairy tale. We have proved that the age-old kind of entertainment based on the classic fairy tale recognizes no young, no old."

—WALT DISNEY

In 1937, with the premiere of *Snow White and the Seven Dwarfs*, Walt Disney and his artists had not only produced a hit movie, they had created the animated feature. Walt Disney observed that *Snow White* also had produced a cultural shift: "I think we have made the fairy tale fashionable again."

Although *Snow White* was an unprecedented success, Walt did not immediately return to the Brothers Grimm or Charles Perrault for fairy

tale material. In fact, it would be more than a dozen years before Disney brought another fairy tale to the screen with *Cinderella* (1950).

Disney and his staff did develop several fairy tales by Danish writer Hans Christian Andersen. Beloved Andersen tales like *The Emperor's New Clothes*, *The Little Fir Tree*, *The Steadfast Tin Soldier*, and *The Emperor's New Nightingale* were interpreted both as individual stories and as a proposed feature-length biography of Andersen. Disney story artist and illustrator Kay Neilsen focused on inspirational sketches and

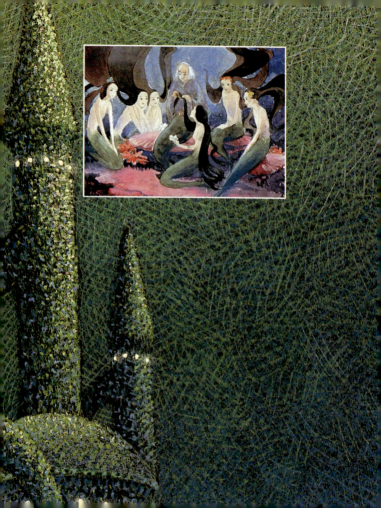

storyboards for another Andersen classic, *The Little Mermaid*.

World War II curtailed development of the Hans Christian Andersen project. In addition, the Disney team encountered daunting story problems. Although steeped in rich fantasy and evocative folklore, Andersen's work also revealed a frequently morose, often pessimistic view of human nature. There was little "happily ever after" in Andersen's tales. So, the meticulous, beautiful, often haunting inspirational art that had been created by the Disney team was carefully filed away.

Theme & Concept

*"The screen version must perceive and emphasize the
basic moral intent and the values upon which every
great persistent fairy tale is founded."*

—WALT DISNEY

In 1985, after completing *The Great Mouse Detective*,
Disney animation writer/director Ron Clements was brows-
ing in a bookstore when he came across Andersen's classic *The
Little Mermaid*. Clements responded to
the story. "It was so cinematic that the
images seemed to leap off the page,"
Clements recalls. Seeing the
tale's potential for animation,
Clements wrote a two-page
treatment for the story and
presented it to the development

team at Walt Disney Feature Animation.

"*The Little Mermaid* was a perfect project for us in that it met our two primary goals: a great story and great characters," says Disney Feature Animation president Peter Schneider. "Being a classic fairy tale, it also had the strong value system and view of the world that has always made Disney animation special." Given the go-ahead to expand the two-page screen treatment, Clements paired up with his co-director/co-writer from *The Great Mouse Detective*, John Musker. Musker, too, was excited by the possibilities inherent in *The Little Mermaid*.

> "*Fairy* tales are usually set in a fantastic landscape, and animation, by the very nature of the medium, can create its own world from scratch."

Together, Clements and Musker worked to get past the intrinsic darkness of the Andersen classic and turn it into a Disney feature. Ironically, it was the same challenge that

had frustrated the Disney staff nearly half a century before. "It is one of the saddest stories ever written," Clements explains. "The biggest problem was with Andersen's ending, where the mermaid sacrifices herself and turns into a sea foam spirit when her love for the Prince is unrequited. We knew we needed a happier ending to really make it work for our purposes. We tried to come up with a way of doing that while somehow remaining faithful to the basic themes of the story." A difficult task indeed, since Andersen's tale is really a Christian parable about earth-bound sacrifice in exchange for immortal life. The film-makers searched for a different theme. They saw that the story also contained elements of a cross-generational con-

flict and a child's need to become an adult, and be responsible for her own choices.

"We hoped the father-daughter subtext would make the movie timeless," Musker says.

Peter Schneider agreed with their philosophical approach. "In *The Little Mermaid*, we have a very powerful theme…that we have to learn to give up our children, to let them be free to do what they want to do—to let them make their own mistakes even though we yearn to protect them. That's universal."

Music

"Through the halls flowed a broad stream, and in it danced the mermen and the mermaids to the music of their own sweet singing. No one on earth has such a lovely voice as theirs. The little mermaid sang more sweetly than them all."
—HANS CHRISTIAN ANDERSEN, *The Little Mermaid*

As Musker and Clements developed the story, composer Howard Ashman was asked if he would contribute to a Disney project. Being a lifelong fan of Andersen, he leapt at the chance to work on *The Little Mermaid*. In the summer of 1986, Musker and Clements met with Ashman and his creative partner, Alan Menken. The songwriters offered myriad observations and opinions on the characters and the evolution of music through the story line, and played an early rendition of a keynote song they had written for Ariel, "Part of Your World." Musker and Clements were dazzled by their work, and Ashman and Menken became an integral part of the creative process of *The Little Mermaid*. In fact, Ashman served as Musker's co-producer for the film.

Ashman and Menken were best known for their Off-Broadway hit *Little Shop of Horrors* (which was being made into a film by Warner Bros.). They emphasized the importance of music in developing characters and telling a story. "In the old days," explains Menken, "the music was written before they began animating. Even some of the background music was written first. In many ways, we've gone back to that tradition for this film by laying the songs out early in the storyboarding process."

"Coming from a musical theater background,"

Ashman explained, "we're used to writing songs for characters in situations.

"*For The Little Mermaid*, we wanted songs that would really move the story forward."

The technique of integrating music into the storyline, rather than using it as background, or having the plot stop cold for a song, evoked images of Broadway classics like *Show Boat* (1927) and *Oklahoma!* (1943).

In addition, the songwriters were happily unencumbered by stylistic conventions.

"*W*orking with a fairy tale, you lose a sense of specific time, and therefore have the latitude to work in all kinds of musical styles,"

Ashman stated. "It allows you to do a different kind of dreaming."

Characters

*"As animators here at Disney, our biggest challenge is not
only to make the characters move, but also to make them
breathe. They have to appear to be thinking and making their
own decisions. You have to see the thinking process.
Whenever I do a scene where that comes across,
then I feel like I've accomplished something."*
—GLEN KEANE, *Supervising Animator, Ariel*

GRIMSBY

The Little Mermaid benefitted from the
Studio's aggressive recruiting of talented
artists. Peter Schneider explained, "Animation
is really a collaborative and repertory artistic
experience. The longer the same people are
together, the better the work becomes.

Mermaid is the beneficiary of five years of training, working, and learning together."

"'Our most important aim is to develop definite personalities in our cartoon characters,' Walt Disney said in 1951, just after the box-office success of *Cinderella* brought happy days back to Disney animation," Peter Schneider relates.

"*Until* a character becomes a personality," Walt said, "it can't be believed, and you have to believe these animated stories."

Andersen's characters were archetypes—none of them even had names. The creative team imbued the character of the little mermaid with the headstrong determination of a typical 16-year-old, and named her Ariel. Although he had gained a reputation for his abilities with powerful and dramatic animation scenes,

supervising animator Glen Keane asked to be assigned to Ariel. "I really wanted a different challenge and a change. I feel as if I grew more on this picture as an artist than I ever have on any other film," Keane said at the time. Keane's inspiration for Ariel was a photograph of his wife that he keeps at his desk. (And although their

appearance is confined to a few scenes, Ariel's sisters were even given individual names—Aquata, Andrina, Arista, Attina, Adella, and Alana—and distinct physical appearances.)

Clements and Musker defined a strong personality for Ariel's father, the sea king, whom they named King Triton. Supervising animator Andreas Deja brought insight into the father-and-child conflict by looking to his own adolescence. "I discovered that there's a lot of my own father in him," Deja

observes. "My father was also very concerned about the fate of his children, and wanted things played by his rules. By thinking back on these confrontations and experiences from my own life, I was able to make things become real."

JETSAM

Musker and Clements expanded the role of the unnamed sea witch from Andersen's story, making her a classic Disney villain, and naming her Ursula. Artists submitted dozens of different designs for Ursula. "We tried Ursula as half-scorpion fish, half-manta ray—finally, we came up with half-octopus," says supervising animator Ruben Aquino. "There's so much you can do with tentacles. They give a creepy feeling."

FLOTSAM

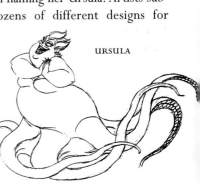

URSULA

169

PRINCE ERIC

The object of Ariel's affection, Prince Eric, was similarly expanded from the dull archetype of the Andersen original into a full-blooded, fun-loving, and romantic young man. "Trying to keep him from being stiff, we made him 'one of the guys,'" Musker says. "We were going for a Jimmy Stewart or Henry Fonda prince…"

New personalities were also created to support the main characters. In Musker and Clements' original treatment,

SEBASTIAN

Ariel had a supervisory liaison to father in the character of a stuffy English conductor-crab named Cecil. Howard Ashman suggested the crab hark from the Caribbean, so the songwriters could experiment with Calypso rhythms. The crab was renamed Sebastian and given an energetic persona. "Sebastian is sort of a reluctant Jiminy Cricket who sees his job of looking after Ariel as being somewhat beneath him," says supervising animator Duncan Marjo-

SCUTTLE

FLOUNDER

172

ribanks. "He has a big ego for such a small body, and he's always in trouble because of his small size." Marjoribanks even studied the real thing for inspiration. "I had a live crab on my desk. But Sebastian doesn't walk sideways—it would be beneath his dignity."

Ariel's childhood companion, Flounder, and a scatter-brained seagull with "expert" knowledge of the human world, Scuttle, were other new characters created for the film.

Environment

"The Little Mermaid *opened up a whole new world that we'd never really experimented with in terms of animation. It's that undersea world, and all the fish and whales and dolphins and mermaids. The creatures all move in a different way, and the animators were enormously excited with it.*"
—ROY E. DISNEY

*S*ince two-thirds of *The Little Mermaid* is set underwater, the production required the creation of a believable aquatic environment. This undersea environment was achieved by a combination of meticulous production and color design, innovative animation techniques, and an abundance of special effects animation.

In the early stages of production, a large aquarium was installed in the Animation Building, and artists frequently gathered to sketch exotic fish, observe their movement, and note the qualities of light and distortion under the water. "Some really nasty things happened down there," Andreas Deja reports. "I mean, things ate other things…or parts of other things. It was a bad mix of fish." As time went by, waves

of aquatic reference photographs from National Geographic and other magazines and reference books drenched the walls of the animators' offices.

"For a fairy tale, we wanted as realistic an environment as possible to make the audience forget it was watching a cartoon," Clements says. The directors turned to a number of visual influences in creating the world "Under the Sea." Cartoonist Rowland B. Wilson influenced the color design with his watercolors of Mediterranean castles and seascapes. The seascapes of Winslow Homer were also studied, and the influence of John Singer Sargent is evident in Prince Eric's castle. Renowned children's book author and illustrator Chris Van Allsburg and veteran Disney layout man Ken O'Connor suggested additional approaches to design.

During this period, the Disney Archives unearthed a package of evocative pastel drawings created by Kay Neilsen nearly 50 years before for the Hans Christian Andersen project. They proved so inspirational that, although Neilsen died in 1957, the filmmakers gave him a screen credit for visual development on *The Little Mermaid*.

With these many inspirations, art directors Mike Peraza and Donald Towns began experimenting with layout, backgrounds, and color to strengthen their support of the story.

"*J*ust because so much of the film takes place under water didn't mean our color palette was limited to blue,"

Towns explained. "We were able to create a full range of moods and emotions by varying and contrasting colors."

To ensure a consistent style and flow of color throughout the film, the art directors created a color script, long, horizontal, multi-paneled boards which sequentially play through the film's scenes from beginning to end. The color script emphasizes color design for each scene and demonstrates how the color designs of the scenes relate to each other. In this dynamic presentation, images progress into each other, showing a contiguous visual flow from scene to scene, and establishing their visual interrelationship.

For the colors of the characters themselves, great care had to be taken to compensate for skin tones and hair color in changing environments and light sources. There were 32 color models for Ariel alone. The Disney paint lab even invented a new color (appropriately named "Ariel") for the blue-green color of her fin.

Character animators, who create realistic, substantial

characters which move with a sense of weight and mass, found themselves a little confused in a liquid world where the laws of gravity simply aren't the same.

"*A*riel's hair almost did us in," recalls one of the mermaid's animators. **"It's very long and thick, and it could move anywhere, any- time. Gravity doesn't apply underwater…and salt water is not the same as fresh water."**

To help animators with this unique environment, an actress was hired to perform many of Ariel's scenes—under- water. The performance, which took place over three days, two in the Glendale YMCA swimming pool, and another day in an eight-foot-deep test tank at Walt Disney Imagineering, was filmed, and the footage was used to help animators acquaint themselves with natural underwater movement.

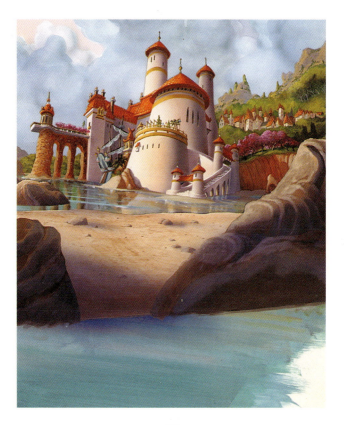

179

While character animation rightfully occupies the spotlight of *The Little Mermaid*, the subtle efforts of the effects animators are important in creating an overall sense of credibility. "This film has more effects than probably any film since *Fantasia*," explains effects animation supervisor Mark Dindal.

"Nearly 80 percent of the film required some kind of effects work."

For research and inspiration, Dindal and his team turned to the 1940 classic *Pinocchio,* in particular the scenes of Pinocchio's underwater adventures with Monstro the whale. "That particular scene really captured the feeling of a massive ocean in terms of its scale and dimensions," says Dindal. "We also discovered how effective the use of distortion effects, bubbles, and light patterns crawling over rocks could be." In the end, a team of 25 effects artists animated sea storms, billowing sails, schools of fish, shadows, raging fire, explosions, pixie dust, surface reflections, underwater distortions, ripples, and hundreds of thousands of air bubbles.

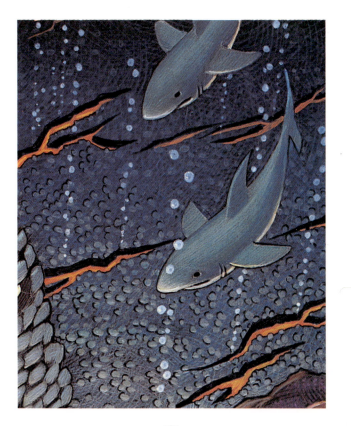

Acclaim

"...Disney's The Little Mermaid *is a jolly and inventive animated fantasy...a movie so creative and so much fun it deserves comparison with the best Disney work of the past....Watching* The Little Mermaid, *I began to feel that the magic of animation had been restored to us... There has been a notion in recent years that animated films are only for kids. But why? The artistry of animation has a clarity and a force that can appeal to everyone, if only it isn't shackled to a dim-witted story.* The Little Mermaid *has music and laughter and visual delight for everyone."*

—ROGER EBERT, *Chicago Sun-Times*

Over the three years of production, *The Little Mermaid* drew on the talents of more than 400 artists and technicians. In the end, nearly 150,000 painted cels and 1,100 backgrounds using more than 1,000 different colors went into making the 7,000 feet of finished film. "We did in a year what they used to do in two to three years," John Musker explains, "by having a bigger staff for a shorter amount of time."

The Little Mermaid had an early premiere in New York and

Los Angeles on November 15, 1989, followed by a general release across North America on November 17.

The public and critical acclaim that greeted *The Little Mermaid* was like nothing the Disney Studios had seen since *Mary Poppins* in 1964. *The Little Mermaid* grossed $84 million in the U.S. and Canada alone—at the time a record for the first release of an animated feature. When the film was released on video in 1990, eight million units were sold in North America alone.

Not surprisingly, the refreshing score for the film was honored with the Golden Globe Awards for Best Song ("Under the Sea") and Best Score.

On Oscar® night, 1990, *The Little Mermaid* swam away with two Academy Awards®, again Best Song ("Under the Sea") and Best Original Score. Another song from the film, "Kiss the Girl," had also been nominated for an Oscar that night. The original soundtrack recording of the songs and score of *The Little Mermaid* also won two Grammy® Awards, Best Song Written Specifically for a Motion Picture or Television ("Under the Sea") and Best Recording for Children, as well as a platinum record for sales in excess of a million units.

The Little Mermaid began a renaissance of the animated art form for the young team at Walt Disney Feature Animation, and led to the staggering artistic and financial successes of *Beauty and the Beast* (1991), *Aladdin* (1992), *The Lion King* (1994), *Pocahontas* (1995), *The Hunchback of Notre Dame* (1996), and *Hercules* (1997). *The Little Mermaid* marked a proud new beginning, built on an impressive and intimidating legacy. It truly signaled the beginning of a second golden age of feature animation for The Walt Disney Studios.

Credits

Produced in Association with
Silver Screen Partners IV

Written and Directed by
John Musker and
Ron Clements

Produced by Howard
Ashman and John Musker

Original score by
Alan Menken

Songs by Howard Ashman
and Alan Menken

DIRECTING ANIMATORS
Mark Henn
Glen Keane
Duncan Marjoribanks
Ruben Aquino
Andreas Deja
Matthew O'Callaghan

ART DIRECTION
Michael A. Peraza, Jr.
Donald A. Towns

VISUAL EFFECTS SUPERVISOR
Mark Dindal

ASSOCIATE PRODUCER
Maureen Donley

SUPERVISING EDITOR
John Carnochan

STORYBOARDS
Roger Allers

Gary Trousdale
Matthew O'Callaghan
Ed Gombert
Thom Enriquez
Joe Ranft
Brenda Chapman

CHARACTER ANIMATORS
Michael Cedeno
Rick Farmiloe
Shawn E. Keller
David Pruiksma
Dan Jeup
Phil Young
Anthony DeRosa
David Cutler
Nik Ranieri
Dave Spafford
Jay Jackson
Barry Temple
James Baxter
Kathy Zielinski
Jorgen Klubien
Chris Bailey
Tony Fucile
Chris Wahl
Chuck Harvey
Tom Sito
Will Finn
Doug Krohn
Leon Joosen
Russ Edmonds
David P. Stephan
Ellen Woodbury
Ron Husband
David A. Pacheco
Tony Anselmo
Rob Minkoff

LAYOUT SUPERVISOR
David A. Dunnet

LAYOUT
Rasoul Azadani
Fred Cline
Lorenzo E. Martinez
Daniel St. Pierre
Bill Perkins
James Beihold

BACKGROUNDS SUPERVISOR
Donald A. Towns

BACKGROUNDS
Jim Coleman
Brian Sebern
Robert Edward Stanton
Cristy Maltese
Doug Ball
Greg Drolette
Tia Kratter
Lisa L. Keene
Philip Phillipson
Andrew Richard Phillipson
Dean Gordon
Craig Robertson
Kathy Altieri
Dennis Durrell

EFFECTS ANIMATORS
Dorse A. Lanpher
Randall Fullmer
Mark Myer
Dave Bossert
Jeff Howard
Christine Harding
Ted C. Kierscey
Don Paul
Kelvin Yasuda
Glenn Chaika
Barry Cook
Chris Jenkins
Eusebio Torres

LAYOUT ASSISTANTS (cont'd)

Marc S. Christenson
Jennifer Chiao-lin Yuan
Mac George
Rene Garcia
Dan McHugh
Roxy Steven

ASSISTANT EFFECTS ANIMATORS

Dan Chaika
Allen Blyth
Mabel Gesner
Craig Littell Herrick
Steve Starr
Mark Barrows
Margaret Craig-Chang
Tom Hush
Mike Nguyen
Allen Stovall
John Tucker

COMPUTER ANIMATION

Tina Price
Andrew Schmidt

COMPUTER ANIMATION ENGINEER

Mary Jane Turner

AIRBRUSH

John Emerson
Bill Arance

EFFECTS GRAPHICS

Bernie Gagliano

ASSISTANTS

Sue Adhopez
Judith Barnes
Kent Culotta
Teresa Eidenbock

Broose Johnson
Kaaren Lundeen
Terry Naughton
Dana M. Reemes
Michael Show
Peggy Tonkonsy
Debra Armstrong
Carl A. Bell
Margie Daniels
Michael A. Genz
Nancy Kniep
Brian McKim
David Nethery
Maria Rosetti
Alan Smart
Alex Topete
Marcia Kimura Dougherty
Terrey Hamada Legrady
Kathleen M. Bailey
Christopher Chu
Lee Dunkman
Ray Harris
Steve Lubin
Mike McKinney
Brett Newton
Natasha Selfridge
Dan Tanaka
Jane Tucker

BREAKDOWNS/ INBETWEENS

Francesca Allen
Jerry Lee Brice
James A. Davis
Mark Fisher
Peter A. Gullerud
Patrick Joens
Tom Mazzocco
Ginny Parmele
Mike Polvani
Bruce Strock
Marianne Tucker

Dave Woodman
Scott Anderson
Sheila Brown
Eileen Dunn
James Fujii
Karen Hardenbergh
Jason Lethcoe
Cynthia Overman
Eric Pigors
William Recinos
Juliet Stroud
Tuck Tucker
Merry Kanawyer Clingen
Dorris Bergstrom
Lee Crowe
Tom Ellery, Jr.
Daniel A. Gracey
Tim Ingersoll
Teresa Martin
Don Parmele
Brian Pimental
Stan Somers
Michael Swofford
Jim van der Keyl
Susan M. Zytka

COLOR MODELISTS

Cindy Finn
Christina Stocks
Brigitte Strother
Linda Webber

COLOR MODEL PAINTERS

Betsy Ergenbright
Carolyn Guske
Linda McCall

COLOR MODEL DEVELOPMENT

Barbara McCormack
Jill Stirdivant

XEROGRAPHIC PROCESSORS

Leyla C. Amaro
Douglas E. Casper
Warren Coffman
Diana Dixon
Suzanne Inglis
Marlene Burkhart
Karen China
Bob Cohen
Kathy Gilmore
Cynthia Neill Knizek
Catherine F. Parotino

MARK-UP

Gina Wootten

XEROGRAPHIC CHECK/ INKING

Kris Brown
Eleanor Dahlen
Eve Fletcher
Anne Hazard
Robin D. Kane
Charlene Miller
Laura Craig
Maria Fenyvesi
Peggy Gregory
Darlene Kanagy
Karan Lee-Storr
Kitty Schoentag
Tatsuko Watanabe

PAINT LAB SUPERVISOR

Debra Y. Siegel

MIX & MATCH

Wilma L. Guenot
Ann Neale

DISPENSARY

Jim Stocks

S. Ann Sullivan
Shannon Fallis-Kane

FINAL CHECK

Monica Albracht
Bonnie Blough
Deborah Mooneyham
Ann Oliphant
Madlyn O'Neill
Howard F. Schwartz
Pat Sito

CEL SERVICE

Jessie A. Palubeski
Florida M. D'Ambrosio
Rose DiBucci
Frances Moralde
Teresita M. Proctor

PAINTING SUPERVISORS

Ginni Mack
Penny Coulter
Barbara Hamane

ASSISTANT SUPERVISORS

James "J.R." Russell
Janette Hulett

MARK-UP/PAINT CHECKERS

Jan Browning
Chuck Gefre
Rhonda L. Hicks
Saskia Raevouri
Ann Sorensen
Susan Burke
Maria Gonzalez
Tanya Moreau
Heidi Shellhorn
Annette Vandenberg

PAINTING

Renee Ilsa Alcazar
Phyllis Bird
Mimi Frances Clayton
Elena Marie Cox
Jean A. DuBois
Etsuko Fujioka
Eadie Hofmann
David Karp
Annette Leavitt
Teri McDonald
Chris Naylor
Melanie Pava
Marilyn Pierson
Bonnie Ramsey
Colene Riffo
Gary G. Shafer
Rose Ann Stire
Cookie Tricarico
Irma Velez
Joyce Alexander
Russell Blandino
Chris Conklin
Sybil Cuzzort
Phyllis Fields
Paulino Garcia
Gina Howard
Kathlyn Kephart
Denise A. Link
Debbie Mihara
Belle Norman
Patricia Pettinelli
Ronna Pincus
Linda Redondo
Nellie B. Rodriguez
Sheryl Ann Smith
Roxanne M. Taylor
Helga Vanden Berge
Hélène Vives
Lada Babicka
Tania Burton
Patti Cowling

PAINTING (cont'd)
Sharon M. Dabek
Joyce Frey
Karen Hepburn
Melody Hughes
Leslie Kober
Ashley Shurl Lupin
Stephanie Myers
Barbara Palmer
Bruce Phillipson
Gale A. Raleigh
Sharon Rehme
Ania Rubisz
Fumiko R. Sommer
Pattie A. Torocsik
Britt van der Nagel
Cathy Walters
Kathy Day Wilbur
Lee Wood
Susan Wileman
Micki Zurcher
Celeste McDonald-Perry

Denise Wogatzke
David J. Zywicki

ADDITIONAL PAINTING
SERVICES
Pacific Rim Productions, Inc.

PAINTING SUPERVISOR
Bethann McCoy

FLORIDA STUDIO TOUR
INK & PAINT
Fran Kirsten
Andrew Simmons
Greg Chin
Robert Kerr
Pam Manes
Lisa Reinert
Elsa Sesto
Pam Vastbinder
Loretta Weeks
Al Kirsten

Jason Buske
Janet English
Mike Lusby
Monica Mendez
Laurie Sacks
Joann Tzuanos
Sharon Vincent
Victoria Winner
Irma Cataya

LIVE ACTION REFERENCE
Sherri Lynn Stoner
Joshua Finkel

Based on the fairy tale by
Hans Christian Andersen

Color by Technicolor®
Prints by Technicolor®

Titles and Opticals by
Cinema Research Corp.

Acknowledgments

My gratitude and affection to Wendy Lefkon and Monique Peterson at Hyperion, and to David Andrew and Sasha Goodman.

As always, thanks to the indispensable Walt Disney Archives: Dave Smith, Robert Tieman, Becky Cline, and Collette Espino.

Thanks to Kevin Ackerman, John Canemaker, David Collins, Jean Cress, Gino De Young, Tim Greer, Richard Jordan, Dan Long, Sean Markland, Kenneth Martinez, Armistead Maupin, Joe Morris, Tim O'Day, Michael Pellerin, Betsy Richman, Dave Walsh, and Gilles C. Wheeler.

And to my biggest fans and best supporters, Mom, Dad, Ron, Joan, Jesse, Darby, Jerry, Shawna, and our merry matriarch, Grandma Mick.